The Surreal Tale

Published by Avani at Kindle

Table of Contents

Acknowledgements

I would like to thank my mother **Vatsala M** who believed in my work and supported me in many ways. This book wouldn't be even exist if my friends hadn't pushed me and ignited the zeal in me to write a book. I take the privilege to thank my friend **Sathvika Venkatesh** and **Sushma K** without whom this book would be concealed just in my mind and wouldn't have reached anyone. The beauty of this book is hidden warmly in **cover** which was **designed by Sushma K**. I would like thank again Sushma K for being with me on this journey from the beginning to the very end.

To be continued

Flashboards in USA's local streets with a authors picture and her recent book .It wasn't surprising that a book launch made news in USA. It always holds good to say authenticity hidden in every book can never be replaced by any digital media.

A recent amateur multitalented personality had driven the attention of media through her excellent skilled hands. She had won hattrick best seller award for her last 3 novels and is now creating havoc of curiosity with her next book launch which was launched previous week.

Her book was planned to be reviewed that Sunday in the auditorium of University of Chicago. Apart from University students ,media and press folks were invited for this event.

On the stage of the review of the of **"A Surrendered Life"** …announcer announces "Let's give big applause for our best selling author Anisha."

Anisha is the **mother** of her **8-year-old** daughter **Anika**…also called as **Anu**. She is a **doctor** by profession and **novelist** by choice. Her surgical skills are as profound as her writing skills. She is known as "**The empathetic healer**"

Anisha takes the mic and …" Thanks for the opportunity yet again .Today in this book launch trailer I would like to say in brief gist of curiosity of why should you read it …I am sure many are curious and excited so let me not leave any minute idle. This book is a extremely special to me. It talks about my vivid imagination. I am not just a writer here ... I am the actor, audience as well .I am the story itself...I am everything!"

There is long pause and Anisha just stops and stares at the big crowd of audience as if she was lost in her own thoughts.

Backstage **director** whispers "Hey! Manoj what is Anisha blabbering? Is this book her biopic? Is she just telling right now some white lies to keep the momentum of being the best? ".

Manoj is as baffled as others "I don't know Charles!! ".

Manoj is Anisha's PA who is her guardian , bodyguard in whole a family member.

Charles: "Stop her right now! We are around the media. We are supposed to have proofs to whatever we tell."

Enraged **Charles** just grabs another mic…"Hey! All Pardon me for disturbance.
I apologise to you all, we have an unforeseen emergency. We promise to reschedule the review soon. Anisha, please go backstage."

Anisha hears the director. Suddenly she is brought back to reality and assumes something happened at home. She rushes backstage sweating as if she ran a 100 m race in 30 sec. Anisha keeps family her top priority. She is typical Indian origin mother after all.

She runs to her green room where Manoj was already waiting for her.
Anisha: "Manoj! What happened? Is my kid alright?". Anisha sighs.

Manoj smiles back confirming that everything was alright. Anisha reaches back home with an unfinished book read session.

Read the Unread Pages

Next day at Anisha's house

On a sofa, Anika is playing with her new toy gifted by Anisha's close friend and watching her favourite cartoon hero "**Chhota Bheem**". While Anisha in the kitchen washing some teacups.

Anisha: "Anu baby! You need to get ready for school. Come here baby! I'll braid your hair"

Anu: "No way Amma! It's still 8 am I have time to get ready!! Kalia ,Dolu and Molu are up to something amma ...Chutki is spying on them....Bheem should come anytime Amma! I can't miss this!! "

Anisha: "Ohho! Anu baby, Bheem will do the same thing again tomorrow...it's ok!..Get ready Anu! Today I can't drop you to your school if you miss your school bus. Fast baby !! Don't trouble your Amma please".

Anu sulks as her mom didn't bear with her tantrums. Anisha knows her kid very well, her sulking is just a matter of another 2 mins post which she will start "her, being back as Anu again".

Anisha makes her hair. Puts on her tiffin and bottle ..."Manoj Ji, please drop Anika to the school van."

Manoj : "Yes, Madam coming..."

Anisha gets ready. The nostalgic look on her face is very evident as she dresses up in her black gown.
She had a planned meeting with her very old college friend cum family Vani.

Vani and Anisha are more than any kit-kin relation. Anisha shares everything with Vani, it's needless to say that the most exclusive details of this best-selling author and the passionate doctor will be known by Vani. Vani is the most caring, loving family to Anisha.

In the cafe,

Vani and Anisha hug tightly as soon as they find each other.They looked into each others eyes as if the extreme happiness would burst out in tears and both are trying not to show that to other one. It is a live scene of famous "Long time no see " moment.

Vani: "Heyy Anisha! How are you and your munchkin doing? It's been so long...I have been missing you both"

Anisha: "I am fine now !!!Infact more than fine!!!I missed you so much. I am so glad you are here travelling miles together all the way from India to USA. How are you? How is your husband? "

Vani: "Yes, Indeed I had to when my friend is extremely busy with her dual profession (winks at Anisha jokingly) …Hahaha!!I am doing just fine! and my husband is as usual. Hahaha!!And if you ask his humour sense don't bother his jokes will never improve, I gave up hahaha !!!"

Anisha and Vani burst into laughter.

Vani: "And yes I see you are in headlines again with your new book and the astonishing part is the media says this book could be your biopic.I am yet to read it......frankly I was a little taken aback is this book a bridge to your life bae yes I may be wrong but...".A worrisome silence in air as Vani stops her sentence mid-way.

Anisha: " Yes, Didn't I say my life is going to be the most blockbuster thing to read if there was a book on me...it's my story in the book."

Vani adds "But...... I mean it's private to you and ..”….Vani stops her sentence midway and diplomatically answers her to show Anisha that she wasn't worried.

Vani adds "Indeed! It will be a hit of course. If you are happy to write I am happy to hear the same...now tell me about this book in detail I am all ears !!"

Vani belongs to an elite family and has connections across politics, media etc...yet Anisha doesn't seek help for any of her book publicity etc. Anisha has a small world in that one of them was Vani who is a friend, a mother, a father, a daughter, and a grandmother too.

Anisha opens up her book...where each word was from the corners of her soft soul and every page was the tissues and bones of her body. She feels the book as if it has life...

Appearances are Deceptive

The book has become the protagonist of this story. Anisha opens the first chapter as they sip coffee…looks into Vani's eyes ......she doesn't have to read her book as this time she is the book herself ...she begins slowly ..."It's a story of a girl in her early 20s Anaya.

Anaya is a fun-loving girl. She has her swag to be stupid and smart too. She is self-made with her choices or chances. The decisions of her life are her turf in her life. She is the master of herself no one could control her.

Vani stops "Ok, so you called yourself Anaya? But is this not the name we gave… So if you used your nickname let me guess then I would be called Roohi if I'm not wrong?"

Anisha adds "Yes, You don't have patience, do you? Haha! Shall I continue now ?"

Vani laughs and nods giving agreement that she can continue.

Anisha continues: "This was about her briefest intro I can think of.

It's a flashback now.

The year 2009

Anaya was a meritorious student and gained a scholarship and a seat in MBBS college by her intellect and passion. She is very contented in her life and needs no one (intending any love hate or sex relation) as she felt "**Relationships complicate things** "

Date 03-06-2009

On the first day of her college, she was sitting in a corner in her lemon-yellow salwar suit reading a book "**Stories of Puranas**".It's a mythological and spiritual book. After a while, 2 more girls approach the same bench.

One with a scarf around with a complete tomboyish look and next to her was another girl with a similar style. Both were twin sisters - **Roohi and Pihu**

The twins stared at Anaya giving a perfect angry glare.Anaya stares back wondering why ? She notices the 2 girls had faded Name Tag which read Roohi and Pihu.

Roohi adds " Get up you Weasley lady this is our bench".Anaya gets enraged
Anaya replies "How is that? You are also the first year and today is the first day. And moreover is there any proof …excuse me ! don't boss over me like this."

Roohi adds "Heyy lady, looks like you have forgotten your manners at home ".Roohi points fingers at the names engraved on the bench which read "**Roohi&Pihu**"

Anaya is shocked.**Pihu** adds "How was that macho woman ? It's our names shall I give you magnifying glasses."

Back in the cafe,

Vani burst into laughter and adds "You were so tomboyish Anisha!! God save us from this woman...haha!!Just kidding. By the way, it was refreshing. "

Anisha adds "Indeed I was . Ohh yes just slipped from my mind when is the ETA of Swara we have to reach before. Swara informed me she would reach home directly"

Vani adds "She should be there by 6 pm evening. Ok!Anisha, we have another 150 mins and I am super curious to hear it's good to go back in days "

Anisha giggles and nods in agreement.

Back to story

Anisha continues …After this heated conversation, Anaya decides to step back as her magazines are empty and bullets have backfired.

Later she gets information that the twins have a year back due to some reason.

At afternoon lunchtime both twins get up and stare at Anaya.Roohi and Pihu decide to reconcile with Anaya as they felt it was for their best. Anaya was also one among the freshers and Roohi intended to get support from freshers so that she and Pihu could be the leaders of the class.Both approach Anaya…

Roohi - " Anaya right ?. Do you want to join us? We know good places."

Anaya - "Yes, People call me **Anaya** .I don't spend like that Roohi. You might have been born with a silver spoon I have not. Sorry! But I can't join "

Roohi and Pihu were taken aback.....Neither they have been blessed as an elite kid.Behind their right hand, they had a tiffin box too.

Roohi: "Hey! Wha...".**Pihu** stops Roohi and says to Roohi "let her be".With pale faces both leave.

The trio judged each other the way they wanted and misunderstood each other.

Anaya – A Hindustani Naari

Every friendship starts with a rough start. The same Roohi, Pihu and Anaya later were nicknamed "**Chitrakoots**".Their friendship stood strong to find peace in their respective lives. They were college queens, the dons and pranksters who enjoyed their respective lives in the company of each other.

Chitrakoot is a famous place where Rama, Laxman and Seeta spent 12 years with peace, hence they called themself Chitrakoots!

Roohi, Pihu and Anaya made a lot of memories throughout their degree. They pranked the teacher once with a cadaver speaking in the lab and freaked everyone....the very next day they kept dirt-covered finger bone in a classmate's bag. She freaked out and threw the same bone away that she got for her experiment in the lab...and Pihu who forgot to get the bone ...picked up thrown bone and reached the lab for practical...The list is long...

The year 2015

The Chitrakoots graduated and finally left their adda(college) of their pranks.Anaya was not interested to do an MD. She wanted to open a clinic with a graduate medical practitioner and start earning. She was looking for an internship in the hospital to gain experience and earn.

Roohi and Pihu were **tomboys** from the beginning they had a great rapport with guys ...unlike Anaya ..she kept her 1ft distance from any attraction and friendship towards opposites.

Among **Chitrakoots** - Anaya was the **Seeta** - a typical Indian woman who believed love is complicated and her society and family respect is the primary part of her character.

Empathy – Strength v/s Weakness

Anaya joined a hospital as a general physician intern. She had excelled in her passion to be a doctor but had one problem she was extremely **empathetic** to her patients which made her hands slow. She used to examine every patient as her own family with utmost care. Her seniors advised her not to speak more than a minute with any patient.

Her happiness was that **HOPE** that she could see in her patient's eyes.
She became a well-known doctor in no time.

One day evening, she gate-crashed a TA (Traffic Accident) patient while she was just about to leave home.

A **male** around age **30** smeared in blood. He had **injured** his **head** and some parts of his **abdomen**.

Anaya was informed to be rushed to ER (casualty). She was dumbstruck to see this horrifying sight. It was her first time to face a critical patient in the last one month of her internship… she took a step back…with low tone feebly whispers "I can't do this please call a senior surgeon...pulse and BP has dropped too much he has to be rushed to OT (Operation Theatre) page Dr. Prabha soon else we will lose him to coma."

Dr. Prabha is a neurosurgeon in the same hospital and Anaya's close buddy in the hospital.

The **Nurse** calls ..."Hello, doctor Nurse Tina from ER. We have a TA patient. Dr Anaya is here but she insisted to page you"

Dr. Prabha " Ok calm down hand over the phone to Anaya I will speak with her". Tina gives the phone receiver .**Dr Prabha** "Anaya tell me the current status of TA patient I need at least 45 mins to reach the hospital till then you got to manage or check if any other senior is available"

Anaya: " At the moment I am there the other in-charge duty doctor has left on emergency call from his family and rest of neurosurgeons I am not able to reach. And yes.....**Status** is....she shivers and tears drop from her eyes which would tell aloud she is nervous and extremely scared as she says...**BP 50/90...pulse is dropping...he is in a mental stupor** (unresponsiveness from which a person can be aroused only by vigorous, physical stimulation)**...Age approx 30....I can see some edema on the right side of the neck region**
The forehead has an external injury and bleeding. The abdomen has an internal injury. I am suspecting there is a spleen rupture. I have taken care of the bleeding from external injuries. But I am afraid in no time he will suffer from breathing issues. And the general surgeon isn't available now suppose it complicates to hemoperitoneum (accumulation of blood in walls of the abdominal cavity) then we need to do laparoscopy......"

Prabha puts a big break to this tense environment.

Prabha adds "Heyyy Anaya hold on! Listen to me carefully...You don't know anything yet .... don't consider the worst scenarios think of better ones .... have you taken a CT scan. If not take now CT of brain and abdomen. I will guide you don't worry!!! I am on my way. Book an OT for 3 hrs and yes if laparoscopy is needed, I will perform it and save his life you don't panic if you panic ...patient will be in danger Anaya try and understand I know you are empathic but here your feelings have no importance against a person's life you got to make right choices. I'll call back in 5 mins by then book OT and check if we have adequate blood, we may need it. I'll tell you for the first and last time. **Your empathy should be your strength, not weakness.** Hurry now without wasting time! "

Anaya hears this statement in her mind "Your empathy should be your strength not weakness " ...."Right choices" ..."Don't panic" repeatedly she is stuck with the receiver in her hand still while the call ended a long time ago.

Tina calls “Dr Anaya what did Dr Prabha say ? will she come? Dr Anaya, are you listening?”

Anaya is brought back to reality..." uhhh......sorry I was .... yes Nurse Tina she is coming." Calls the OT in charge…"Hello, we need an OT for 3 hrs. We will start in the next 1 hr once Dr Prabha reaches the hospital."

OT in-charge confirms that OT NO 8 is available in the next 30 mins and confirms that the anaesthesiologist of the previous operation is made to stay back since she is free for the next 4 hrs until her next OT duty. Anaya is relieved and she eagerly waits for Prabha to call back. She feels that those few mins were the longest time in her entire life.

Slaves of Heart and Hostage of Mind

Anaya gets busy with her patient…she instructs Nurse Tina to get a **brain and abdomen** CT, while she waits for Dr. Prabha to call back standing right next to the patient.

Just then she feels something weird happening to her….. someone is touching her right hand…with a hopeful wish …she turns to find her patient conscious. It was a **dream come true** for her to see him awake. She comes closer and examines if he is responding to her actions and asks him his name. He says in a feeble voice that reads "AE8007" , Anaya is flabbergasted…she tries to think again and again about what was he conveying to her.

After some time, she recalls he had met with an accident by a head-on collision with a car and he could be conveying the license number of the culprit's car. By then he loses consciousness ...

Nurse Tina conveys that the patient's vitals have stabilised now ….Anaya is sceptical on loss of consciousness again which is not good according to her medical know-hows, she starts anticipating suppose there are more critical internal injuries in the brain. She waits for the CT scan reports outside the lab eagerly. She doesn't realise that 5 mins have long gone and she still feels Dr. Prabha will call her back in 5 mins.

Dr Prabha always makes a statement during her teachings "**Moral support is most effective after all we are slaves of heart and hostages of mind**"

Dr Prabha knew well what is Anaya's capability that was the very reason she assured that she will call back in 5 mins as she knew all Anaya needed was to know there is moral support intact who believes in her talent.
Dr Prabha needed another 15 mins to reach the hospital.

Just then police team comes in to find out the status of the patient since it's a TA it was obvious to inform the police. Anaya turns to the police inspector at door and walks towards him ….the police inspector rushes to the bed passing her ...with worry written all over his face.

Anaya turns and looks at the inspector . He sees the unconscious patient and returns back in the next second to Anaya to ask about the status of her patient.

Anaya conveys that the patient vitals are stabilised but he needs to be kept monitored.

Just then Anaya gets the report from the lab and she could clearly see "**cerebral edema**" (swelling in the brain) but thankfully there were no spleen rupture or internal abdominal injuries.

Anaya rushes to the ward. She now knows she got to **induce hypothermia** (Lowering body temperature) to reduce the intracranial pressure ie pressure among the brain blood vessels.

She injects an **Anticholinergic drug** which aids the same. Also adds an oxygen concentrator until the brain swelling reduces, body has to get adequate blood and oxygen else the organs fail in no time. Anaya has a unique quality to prepare for the worst though the chances of him being relived are high from the treatment she provided yet she prepares the OT to perform **ventriculostomy** (A procedure to drain out the fluid in the brain). Just in-case if edema doesn't reduce she would be ready to do the next step in Plan B.

For a doctor right treatment is not one that their medical book teaches it's the one that the body welcomes as always the human body remains a never solved beautiful mystery.

The inspector realises that reports of TA patient had come up.

He rushes to Anaya to enquire same "What happened? Is he alright? "

Anaya replies to him with contented smile "Yes he is fine and should be better in some time hopefully...but there is some swelling in the brain so we have to watch out for his acceptance to the treatment given right now to reduce the swelling ".She informs the letters blabbered by him to the inspector as she leaves the ward to her cabin which is next to ER.

Anaya recalls the day when she first gave first-aid CPR to revive the heartbeat of one of the emergency patient...missing her theory subject exams during her medical course for an old man who collapsed with myocardial infraction when she just got down bus in front of her college ".That day she saved herself as a medical student and her patient.

After 2 hrs Nurse Tina rushes to Anaya's cabin. Anaya is shocked to see Tina's worrisome face assumes that her patient could be in danger. She was always known for extreme empathy and sensitive nature........though she was prepared for the worst but she didn't want to perform surgery. There is a saying something very similar
"If a treatment doesn't have side effects then it didn't work too"

Surgery implies some more variables that can happen post-surgery. Anaya always hoped to treat her patient without surgery.

Nurse Tina takes long breaths continuously and adds "Dr Anaya, Patient Siddarth Singh is conscious now and is looking for you".**Anaya** gasps "What! That's a relief why did you rush like this you almost gave me a heart attack!"

By then Dr Prabha reaches the hospital to find Anaya has done her job perfectly. Dr Prabha and Anaya have a short chat about the patient.
Anaya wore broad smile on her face and felt it was a meaningful day. Dr Prabha walks to her cabin wearing a proud smile on her face as if she knew what would happen long before.

Trust is key to a lot of treasures!

Siddarth -A Techie

Anaya reaches the ER (Casualty) to check on patient...."Yes, How are you? Do you feel dizzy, or nauseous? "

Siddarth: "Sorry! I heard I had woken up briefly did I say anything? I can't remember now ".

Anaya: "Yes, you conveyed to me ...and it appeared to be like a license plate number of the culprit who crashed your car. I have conveyed the same with that person standing over there" She directs the finger over the reception desk afar where the inspector was standing impatiently, apparently the news of Siddarth didn't reach the police team"

Anaya checks the chart and finds now the name of the patient was "Siddarth Singh " just to realise how absent-minded she was .....all along she didn't even check the patient's name.

The chart was attached with the police report with personnel details. It stated he was a Software engineer in an MNC.A white-collar job!

As he catches sight of inspect he feels relieved and turns to Anaya to ask what was it he conveyed then. Anaya repeats the number and also conveys that as a side effect of the treatment or the injury he might have memory flashes now and then but they will eventually stabilise and everything would be back to normal. Siddarth listens to the number carefully and thanks the doctor for remembering the numbers.

Anaya is shell shocked to hear that his gratitude was not towards saving his life but to remember the number of hit and run person's car.

Anaya repeats again that he has suffered moderate risk edema in the brain which is reducing but he has to take proper care while it heals...expecting this time he would thank her for saving his life. But to her vain, he replies back "Hmm"
Anaya now gets impatient with a stern voice she replies "I think you forgot something ... Shouldn't you at least assure me to obey me at the very least... forget thanking"

Siddarth: " Ohh! So sorry didn't realise! I will do everything that you mentioned now but yes catching that hit-and-run guy is the most important thing to me right now...I have to punish him, isn't it? He nearly killed me."

Anaya feels that he did have a point and realises that it was too much to be expecting from a patient…afterall he was someone who suffered a trauma .She leaves the ward with a warm smile and pats his back conveying "I second that"

Anaya leaves home.

In the hospital

Inspector Rawat gets the news and rushes to Siddarth.

Rawat is a close friend-cum family of Siddarth Singh.

Rawat: "Are you ok sir ?"

Siddarth: " Yes brother, I am better. I heard the doctor conveyed to you the license plate number. And please let's not be so formal when I just came back being dead" smiles jokingly.

Rawat smiles agreeing with him and replies "Ok! Sid, I will get back to you soon "

Siddarth makes a telephone call to his office and conveys he is hospitalised and will take up the client meeting here.

Nurse Tina who heard all this thinks …" why does he want to take up a meeting when he is in this condition or is he a CEO or something strange guy "

Siddarth turns to Nurse Tina who was adjusting the next bed cover and asks her if they can shift him to a private ward.

Nurse Tina confirms that he would be shifted in the next 1 hour.

She whispers grumbling to herself …"All IT people are weird no wonder".. she recalls her brother working while he was suffering from TB(Tuberculosis).

Hidden Names

Anaya reaches home to find Pihu and Roohi already sleeping on the sofa waiting for her to wish her on her birthday eve.

It was past 12.Anaya never recalls her birthdays it was never important before nor will be any time in future...but one thing she loves about her birthday was this visit that her heartstrings make every year without fail.

At the cafe,

Vani exclaims !! …."Indeed! By the way, today is the same day as your book dates it is your birthday eve and I am sure you don't remember this do you? "

Anisha gets back to present her heart beating like crazy .....after a moment ....gives an innocent smile to Vani nods in agreement

Vani : "Hope you didn't cover our pranks I'll too embarrassed to listen! God!"

Anisha: " I know how to hide. You should know more than anyone."

Anisha realises that her story flow was broken again she angrily tells Vani "You just broke my flow woman !" and giggles

Vani giggles " Yes, because I am hungry it's been 2 hrs ...but indeed felt like going back to college days! Will continue at home today! I am actually pretty excited to hear what might be next …you never know …..I might find some more Achilles heel of you through this ….I am a business woman remember.Haha! By the way, Swara will reaching late she texted now.... she has to do some run errands regarding company things! You know how it is! Uff and we being co-owners it's super hectic "

Anisha adds " Of course! I can understand!My CEO!!! Ok, let's order something very fast and get going it's almost time.Anu will be home by now.If she doesn't find me it will be a nightmare all evening! Haha! And yes soon after she comes home she will have a big story to tell about her day! Today you can hear it too.Haha "

Vani and Anisha bursts into laughter with a rejuvenating. They soon finish their lunch and leave home.

In Anisha's house

Anu is already home when they reach and she is busy searching her Amma to start her story ...just then Anisha enters the front door to hear

Anu screams from the top floor " Amma! Where were you? I searched you so much."

Anisha and Vani look at each other and burst into laughter.
Anisha: "Look who is home? "

Vani " Hello! Baby "

Anu brightly smiles to see her Roohi Aunty home.
Anu adds "Yayy! Let's have fun Roohi Aunty! Where is Pihu Aunty? Why can't I see her?"

Vani: " She will come in another hour baby meanwhile you start your mega story! On your marks get set go! "

Anisha giggles and replies to Vani .."sorry I couldn't train her to say your name she says she likes your hidden nickname sorry what was that code name… Haha!!!."

Vani: " Aree! I always feel embarrassed to hear that kiddish name it's okay as long as Anika calls "

Anika starts her school story by entertaining the duo friends.

In an hour,

Swara knocks on the door.. she exclaims loudly "Ohho ! My lady love where were you all this time! ".

Anisha stares at her turns to Vani and exclaims "Ohho Vani, this woman is still the same ".

Anisha adds " Look who is asking me wrong question ….I should ask you why are you so late madam?".

Swara adds "After all it's your birthday eve today Anaya! I had things to prep for the d-day "

Vani giggles at Anisha.

Anisha turns to Swara "Dare you call me that name! " Pulls Swara's ears and drags her into the living room.

Swara retreats and conveys she won't call her in that name again.

Swara adds "Anyway, I heard the gist of your story so far from Vani. Both of us will be here for next complete week…so can I ask for your locker keys please?..authors make a lot of money don't they ? And yes by the way …while you don't like the name we gave you how come you took our names there! I have been wondering the same!!! "

Anisha giggles and adds " My dictionary went dry! Haha! "

Happy Birthday!

Vani and Swara are also professionally graduated as doctors and the trio's friendship dated back to their early age of youth, love and innocence .They were married to the two sons of **Quest foundation**. Quest foundation owns and has its versatility from clothing to construction. Vani and Swara are Co-owners of one of the Clothings and Cosmetic stores the flag bearers of brand "**Swaragini**" ("Swara"+"Vani") which has its roots all over India and now they have planned to venture abroad markets starting from USA city called Texas.

The twins and Anisha had a great evening thanks to Anu who didn't leave any stone unturned in entertaining them with her stories.

It was past 10 pm, Anu's bedtime

Anisha escorts the twins to their rooms on the top floor along with Anu. The guest rooms and kid's room are architected perfectly that the voices on the lower floor don't reach the floor above. The secrets of the floor below are a mystery to the floor above and needless to say vice versa.

Vani and Swara reach the rooms as they now have 3hrs more to decorate. Twins slowly go to the balcony to decorate the place.

Swara had 2 suitcases. One was her stuff for the next week while the other was entirely dedicated to getting props to decorate the place.

Swara has a very "creative mind" while Vani has excellent "craftmanship in styling and cosmetics and makeover". Hence "Swaragini" is known for its talent in the field well.

In the next one hour

Swara made an arch with flowers **- "Themed -Artistic Aesthetic Of Author"** and Vani stacked books with "**Happy birthday" - The touch of celebrating an author's birthday:)**

H
A
P
P
Y
B
D
A
Y

Swara and Vani both go to their room softly ... changing their outfits to the normal one-piece gowns. Swara in red and Vani in green. They had kept a yellow gown ready for Anisha. On the table, there were 2 masks (Jane Austen and JK Rowling's faces were printed on them)

It was 12 ...the duo slowly comes downstairs and opens Anisha's room…to find Anisha was fast asleep on the bed.

The door's slight crackling sound wakes Anisha she turns around to find Vani wearing a Jane Austen mask and Swara as JK Rowling mask on and dressed in a beautiful gown. **Both** say together "**Happy birthday Anisha** !!!".

Anisha is awestruck as she wakes up from bed….a shy and contented smile on her face was evident but she doesn't reply back. The twins pull Anisha out of her bed asks her to change to the yellow gown and come upstairs. Anisha obeys in the next 15 mins she gets ready and reaches upstairs to find the balcony beautifully decorated leaving Anisha shell shocked yet again.

Anisha runs over the twins and hugs them tightly …tears rolled out of her eyes all the way on her checks as if tears were enjoying a roller-coaster ride ….her gesture spoke more than any gratitude or any cliché exaggerating words to express emotion that would convey. The trio knew what was conveyed and what was received. There is a saying "**Feelings are better expressed than told**" which fits perfectly in this context.

After a brief moment of 30 sec, Swara breaks this momentum and asks Anisha to cut the cake as she was hungry after doing all the hard work :)

Anisha cut the cake and the trio takes a few pictures. Later Anisha brings 3 sleeping bags for them to sleep under the night sky.

The 3 stares at the night sky.

Swara replies "Hey Anisha! Hats off I heard the story was beautifully written and to be frank I felt I am hearing an open dairy of yours... but what made you write this on your life? "

Swara looks at both of them with a puzzled face. Vani gives a calm look conveying all good on her face. **Anisha** replies "Nothing as such told you this author has exhausted her dictionary...Haha! It was an experiment by the way don't worry I have not written about your mischief! Haha"

Swara giggles and says " Had you added them you would have got a big award for literature...Ok enough!enough!!! You continue the story I guess now we have some role in your book in the next chapter ". Swara giggles and turns at Vani winks her eye naughtily.

Anisha giggles "Excuse me! Don't keep your expectation high! Hahaha! And yes slowly you guys are so loud if Anu wakes up …Swara you will be taking responsibility to put her back to sleep"

Swara and Vani keep their finger on their lips and gesture to Anisha to continue her story...with slight giggle on face.

Serious/prank

Anisha continues her story on popular demand from **her** people …**Back to story now** Even that day it was Anaya's birthday eve so ...

At almost 12:01 am, Roohi and Pihu slowly walk as Anaya leaves them undisturbed thinking they were fast asleep.

Both reach Anaya's room go behind the door while Anaya was freshening up ...to her surprise the twins scream "Happy birthday".

Anaya burst into tears watching this beautiful surprise from the duo pair.

Anaya adds "My Chitrakoots, truly you guys are wonderful! I really needed this today."And she briefly explains the whole tense situation that happened in the hospital.

The twins console her and they say they have an announcement to make on this day.

Anaya adds "Really what is it ?".

Roohi adds "You are first to know this! Hold your seats. I and Pihu are in love. I know you are aware of that! But look here (both show the rings) we were proposed together yesterday on a dual date. We both will convey this to our family soon and there will be double "barath" entering our gates Anaya!!! My parents and their parents have already been in agreement when we started to date so it's a matter of deciding dates that's all !!! yippee!!! I am so excited "

Pihu adds "Not just that, And I don't know if we are lucky enough but they both run a business of clothing and cosmetics industry so we will be taking our profession in that direction soon. We are excited that we are finally following our passion."

Anaya's happiness sparkled all over her face …she was extremely elated to hear this wonderful news from her heartstrings….she replies in excitement "OMG!! That's too good! Aree my lovely Chitrakoots you guys made it! I was anxious all this while ….why you guys don't fasten this up! Godman! You guys made it! I am so happy! Yipee! Let's have a tight hug! Come on !!!"

The trio hug each other and they talk all night.It was night filled with laughter , excitement and a whole lot of new dreams. Next day the dawn light touched Anaya's feet to wake her up. Roohi and Pihu were still asleep while Anaya tip-toe to bathroom to freshen up and leaves for the hospital.

She goes to her cabin. Her morning rounds start usually at 9 pm. She accompanies Dr. Prabha as an assistant doctor in charge.

Anaya goes to the nurse station to ask about her patients in the wards and Nurse Tina and her colleagues warmly wish her for birthday with a cake.

It was almost 10 am and the next ward to visit was the TA patient "**Siddarth**".

Nurse Tina, Dr.Prabha and Anaya reach the ward to find it closed and locked inside.

Dr.Prabha gets heated up and yells at Nurse Tina "why is a patient locked up this way who will take responsibility if something happens while he is alone and locked up?"

Dr.Prabha knocks on the doors angrily and hears no response from another end. By then **Nurse Tina** defends and replies "Dr.Prabha, my apologies… I am aware of this he said he has an office meeting at 10 am and needed privacy. Please excuse this mistake . I apologise" she puts her head down in guilt.

This statement enraged **Dr.Prabha** .With a angry tone Dr Prabha "If that's the case I am not visiting this ward today. Anaya since you took care of this patient please follow up and if possible ask him to learn some manners it isn't his house to do as he wishes"

Anaya nods. Dr Prabha leaves the place.**Anaya** asks Nurse Tina "What is this Nurse Tina ? What is this meeting for a person who nearly touched doors of death right a night ago? And monitoring him is crucial and he missed the doctor's checkup right the very next day, now what if things become complicated?"

Nurse Tina adds "Yesterday I heard him saying on the phone he wants to take up client meeting looks like its some important thing from his office.. Excuse him he looks like a hardworking earning hand ."

Anaya cools down after hearing Nurse Tina as she did have a valid point stares at locked door sternly and replies "Page me when this door is unlocked"

Indicating she had no mercy and would be giving her patient an earful of advice. She returns back to her cabin.

Around 11 am it was Anaya's regular OPD time which continues till noon. She did not get any page from Nurse Tina.

Anaya becomes anxious she decides to visit Siddarth's ward as soon as she finishes her OPD irrespective of whether he was free or he is in the washroom or anywhere.

Anaya doesn't want to take chances for him it was her responsibility and he was her patient.

Around noon, as she is about to wrap up OPD she gets a page from Nurse Tina that Ward 103 is open.

Anaya rushes to the floor. As she opens the door **Siddarth** stands and welcomes her with a bright smile and says "Happy birthday my saviour doc"

She is awestruck and puzzled as to how in the world does he know her birthday.

She thanks him and asks him how does he know her birthday.

Siddarth giggles and says he saw her at the nurse station in the morning and also apologises for keeping the door locked.

She is cooled now to see her patient fit enough.She adds "Ok, I am happy you know manners. I needed apologies since you gave one before I asked I accept it. But I don't want you to repeat this mistake again. Since you look fine we will get you discharged in another day or two.But please come for follow up check-up post that as well. I will get your discharge ready sooner."

Anaya looks at the chart and checks his vitals

She adds "Are the police still here? Did they catch the culprit? I didn't see any news of your hit and run case anywhere in today's paper too ..just like that curious "

Siddarth replies " Hahaha! Ok, so the doc is curious too. Yes, the police are still here and won't go until I am discharged because the one in uniform is like a family to me. Uhhh ...yes, they didn't catch the culprit yet..and it is not on the news because :(I am not a news sensational person."

Everything was the same but that day Anaya had smiled. There was a different air between her and Siddarth. He was someone who was now comfortable to speak with. Unknown softness and tenderness layer was being built without Anaya's knowledge.

The next day

Anaya starts her rounds, this time she requests Dr.Prabha that she will take complete ownership of Siddarth. Dr.Prabha who was confident in her agrees.

Anaya gets excited to visit his ward. She rushes to the ward to stand still to find Rawat and Siddarth having a serious discussion and Siddarth was sounded little tensed. Anaya enters as they were talking about the case ...she decides not to talk to him ...checks his vitals and silently leaves. Siddarth makes a calm eye contact smile conveying he was fine.

Almost by noon, Nurse Tina pages Anaya to inform her that Ward 103 Siddarth is requesting a discharge. Anaya is taken aback, she gets puzzled why is this guy a new person every day. She signs and asks Nurse Tina to prepare a discharge summary.

Around 4pm , all the processes were almost done. Siddarth visits Anaya's cabin to find her not available. He enquires the nurse station to find that Anaya was in OT and leaves hospital without visiting his doctor.

Anaya returns to her cabin around evening 6 pm, finishing her OT.

She takes her bag to find a note stuck to her vanity which read " Thank you doc! 3219766234?"

Thank you doc! 3219766234?

She guesses that this note must be Siddarth's.She wonders what in the world was meant by those numbers as it didn't look like a phone number.

Yet Anaya takes in the note.That night she calls up her twins to ask if they knew what this meant.

The trio always jointly does pranks and mischief all the time. Anaya was confident when they were as the power of 3 they would be able to understand anything.

All three note down numbers and would meet again the next night with the results. **Roohi** makes a statement before the call end "A weirdo playing pranks on our queen! Hahaha!!".

Anaya was disturbed, as now she feels why in the world she needs to find what it means?

What is in the book?

In Anisha's home on her birthday eve night ,

Vani exclaims "I remember that day. Uff seriously! It was interesting wasn't it ?".**Swara** agrees and yawns and conveys she was very sleepy.Anisha and Vani giggle and pat Swara to bed and they crawl inside their sleeping bags and have a good night sleep with a calm smiles on their faces which showed the satisfaction of night spent well.

The next morning Anisha wakes up and dresses Anu for school, she rushes to the car to meet the illustrator of her new book that she had finalised and then to the hospital she had OT that day which would take some time.

She bid bye to the twins.At Anisha's home, Swara and Vani clean up the place filled with dried flowers.

As they clean place.**Swara** turns to asks Vani "Do you have any idea why did she write this? Do you think she knows the truth now? And the main mystery is why did she become a writer ? .Did you ever know she had passion in writing ? I have never seen her."

Vani adds "We will know eventually let's complete her book first".Swara nods in agreement.

Swara turns back immediately with bright smile as if she was ready to spurt some weird ideas that occasionally runs in her mind " Vani, Why don't we read the whole book ourselves? Do you know where is the book? Let me find out one copy should be around here."

This time Vani doesn’t stop Swara as she is also somewhere extremely curious on how the book will go.They begin their search …they search living room, study rooms,bed rooms, everywhere but in vain. Later after a long search, Vani finds the book in Anisha's cupboard corner that read "**The Surrendered life**".

Vani screams at the top of voice “Swara I found it! Come down!!”.Swara runs downstairs towards her sister.Vani with smile on her face holds the book and shows Swara.Swara smiles in agreement. Vani looks at the book and says to Swara “But how is it that there is just one book in the whole house hahaha! Looks like the book will indeed be another best seller that the author herself doesn't have a few copies to preserve "

Swara replies "No wonder she didn't share a copy with us. Of course, we never read her books any way she has always read them to us online or offline... Hahaha!"

Both start reading them together from the point where Anisha left last night.

Kit Kat?

In the book, Vani starts to read

Anaya tries to decode for the next 2 days in vain she leaves the hope thinking this must be a prank. Neither her friends could aid in the same.

One day, as usual she wakes up in the morning with the coffee mug in hand and sits in her balcony like every day. She lives on the 2nd floor .It is fun filled sight to see down kids playing every morning …the kids playing. She smiles at them and they smile back and this has become the daily dosage for her.Suddenly she notices the numbers drawn on ground and kids playing the famous game Kit Kat game. Her gut feeling speaks loudly that the missing link of the puzzle has the key in this game.

Then she laughs at herself of being so stupid.She takes her mug off the window pane of balcony and get's up to notice the café "Kit Kat ?". She recalls the game was an activity conducted by the cafe "Kit Kat ?" in their inauguration event and her flat kids were only ones to play in near by area.She recalls her puzzle also had "?".She ponders if this café and the game kit kat had some relation to her puzzle.

She decides to give a try…

The Kit Kat game was very simple. There were numbers 1-9 blocks and 3 kids stood randomly on numbers. 4th kid stands in front turning back - He was called the gatekeeper.

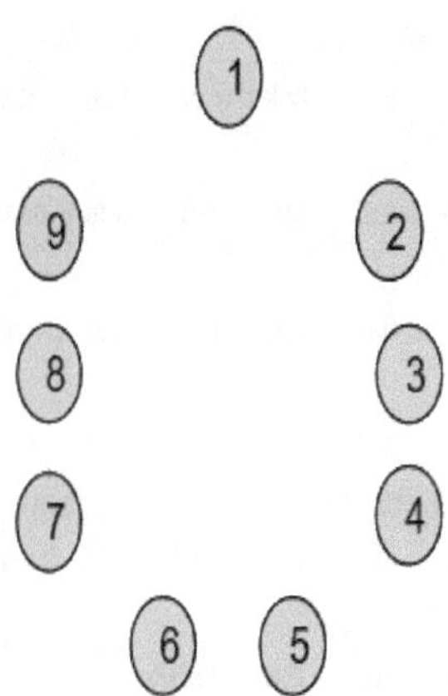

When the gatekeeper says "Kit" the person who stands on a number has to move 3 steps backwards, suppose the kid is standing at number 3, she has to move 9th block and if the gatekeeper says "Kat" kids move 3 steps forwards to number 6 in the same way until they get confused and moves in the wrong direction.. this game continues.

Kit means backwards 3 steps and Kat means forward 3 steps.

Anaya wonders what if 3219766234 I do like ….writes on a paper.

3	2	1	9	7	6	6	2	3	4
Kit	Kat	Kit	Kat	Kit	Kat	Kit	Kat	Kit	Kat
9	5	7	3	4	9	3	5	9	7

It decodes to a number **9573493597**. She now realises after all he shared his phone number in such a complicated manner.

And the note was Thank you doc....phone number and question mark. What does this question mark mean is asking me to call? Or is he asking me to meet at the same cafe?

She realises that Siddarth definitely knew more than what she actually thought.

And decides to ask him herself what and why and how on earth was all this possible.

But she hesitates, what if this number was someone else she might have miscalculated or she was overthinking.

But somewhere her gut screamed that she was right in every way and the note was particularly made so that she was only one who could decode it and no one else.

She decides to call the number to find out if she was really right or not.

Dials the number ...**Anaya** says " Hello ! Can I speak to Siddarth Singh ?"

Siddarth replies back " Hello! That's great you found my number."

Anaya adds "So you also might be knowing I have called to ask for an explanation. Otherwise, I would have texted you the time and date to meet at the venue you mentioned in the note. How in the world you know my home? How do you know that ?"

Siddarth replies back with astonishing tone " Woow! You caught that too. So when are we meeting at "Kit Kat ?" cafe"

Anaya adds "Well, it depends on your explanation of spying on me."

Siddarth replies back with naughty smile " Woow, easy... I didn't stalk you I was passing by doing some errands on the day of my accident near your home…well I was familiar with your face I have seen you around in this neigbourhood multiple times even when you come out in your night wear to buy vegetables as well !! as my house is close by and that's how that day I reached your hospital too since it was close by. I saw the kids play that same Kit Kat game. That's when I saw that cafe ....but unfortunately, on the way going to the same cafe, I met with an accident ...if you don't believe me you can check where was the accident spot. I can assure you I am a decent guy. And yes now can you please tell me when can we meet I want to have an important conversation with you regarding my accident?"

Anaya replies "What would that be you should ask the policemen?

Siddarth Singh: "Can you please come it's important to me ?

Anaya : Ok, I'll assume for now that whatever you knitted is true and I hope it stays the same, I assure you one thing Siddarth if I find that this is a lie I promise you that I won't be as nice as you think of me, of course.If you see me at 7 pm consider that I have believed your tale. "

Siddarth replies in agreement " Yes, Mam .I assure you one thing as well doc ....today is that D-day when you will change perspectives of me that I am not the person you think I am ."

Anaya replies in surprise "Ohh really will know it by end of the day. Hope you don't have trauma after the accident."

Siddarth adds " Of course not, its petty things to me"

Anaya replies in sternly "Accident is not funny and on that injury to the brain is still not funny. So please don't talk as if it's part of your everyday life"

Siddarth replies in agreement" Ok, ma'am, Sorry, my bad I shall obey my doc after all you were my saviour."

Anaya hangs the phone. She is curious and anxious as well.

Evening at 6:30 pm, Anaya leaves the hospital after verifying whether whatever he spluttered was true or not.And to Anaya's surprise, the accident location was the same place.Anaya reaches almost 6:55 pm...to see Siddarth already in the Cafe waiting for her.

She approaches table.Both look at each other in curiousity as if they were conversing with their eyes alone.

Anaya : "So Siddarth what was the reason you called me and why did you have to give me something to decode you could have shared directly if you had anything to speak "

Siddarth adds " Yes, I think you forgot the order…Hello Doc ! How was your OT? Hahaha! Easy doc easy !!will tell you everything ….so you can call me Sid by the way. It was a friendly request to ask you something important. And of course, I gave that number to decode just for fun nothing deep meaning in that. Well I thought I would come to visit you at the hospital had I not received your call in morning."

Anaya replies "Ohhh, do I really have to follow the order. (gives a proud smile) I follow the order I want and yes it depends on whom I am with" (looks at Siddarth sitting on chair while Anaya standing across the table.She adds "I am Dr Anaya, and I am not your friend definitely."

Siddarth gestures her to sit down across with calm smile.

And replies back "Ok, Let's see about other things later… back to why I called you …on a serious note... I want to have this conversation just between us. Can you tell me the day when I came to your hospital, did I have anything that I held tight etc anything you remember"

Anaya adds "Woow, chills if you have lost something please check the lost found section in **OPD**. You didn't have to call me to ask this "

Siddarth replies back nodding his head in disagreement "No No, I am asking…. just asking "

Anaya calms down now .She decides to listen to him and not be judgemental.

Anaya replies "Sorry I was rude ….Ok, but yes the lady who took brought you in seems to be a thug she just left you without saying your condition so there was chaos on your identity **Nurse Tina** said another day. But why any serious problem?"

Siddarth adds "Not sure if I can bring this to you or not, I am a Software professional but there is some dramatic backstory to my life. I am actually searching for a close relative with whom I lost contact during my childhood. That day I felt I saw that person during the collision on the road."

Anaya adds "And so the one who got you could be the same person? then what was that license plate all about? Why are you trying to find that guy when you are desperate for something else?"

Siddarth adds "I think the one who brought me was a mother of a kid who stays in your apartment. She saw my accident closest apparently and brought me to your hospital. And ….yes The car that collided with me was a Benz car that had a black box camera. It's rare that in India a car has a black box camera. So it caught my eyes and its numbers too. I have contacted that guy too to check if anything is captured there unfortunately nothing was captured. Anyway, he will be penalised and unfortunately, I will also be penalised. I broke a signal and took a wrong turn."

Anaya gets irritated now "Ohh Please….you really make stories, don't you? And yes finding your relative doesn't mean you reach heaven before he/she reaches you."

Siddarth adds " On this note! I make stories or films or my words are trailers you will know eventual ... for now let's take cheers on our friendship ....Shall we? Not okay? Okay? to be a friend "

Anaya replies with smile "...ok I mean for a stranger to the patient to a stranger to friend you made a long way. I will give you that though I don't trust you"

Siddarth replies "Easy ...no issues :)"

Both cheer their glasses and laugh out loud. Siddarth's jokes are something Anaya loved that evening.

Martial Courtship

The meeting that started at the cafe, was repeated. They clashed here and there on the way passing by. Sometimes at the hospital for check-ups sometimes in supermart.

The air between them became friendlier.Siddarth never showed special care to Anaya ...the change in inclination was something Anaya felt. It was not from another end. And here things changed ...

By now trio group knew Siddarth too and they and their respective boyfriends.Siddarth knew Anaya's special friendship with the twins.

Anaya was a self-composed woman by choice. She did not want to get deviated from that primarily because she felt being under control she could plan the life she wanted.

She wanted to have a stable job, a family from an arranged relationship which she believed was safest to bet on.

Anaya was definitely a family woman. She had a clear vision that she would have clear control over herself.

An Indian family doesn't just come with the kid when a kid is born ...her Rashi, her caste ... her tradition ...her rules are made to be worn all her life. It's the attire of any person.

Anaya who never spoke to a stranger so openly ...it was her first move that showed Anaya has tilted her inclination somehow.

Anaya's resilience comes from her attitude. The day she realised that somewhere ..she is about to deviate she felt "yes …its high time to bring herself back."

Anaya was at her prime age of 25 and by then her parents were also like anyone looking for a groom. Anaya felt martial courtship was very important.

One day she gets an alliance from the same attire(personified as caste) that she wears.

The person biodata was :

Hari Shetty

Working in MNC, XXX salary.

Anaya is nervous she is exceptional surgeon who can dissect a person and cure his ailment but she was extremely new when it comes to dating people or even talking to man with intension of relationship/marriage.

But as always everyone starts as fresher so she musters courage.

That evening she leaves from hospital for blind date with this man at restaurant. Anaya reaches restaurant to find Hari already waiting for her …She sits across the table. But neither of them start conversation.The silence in air spoke louder than normal and Anaya couldn't bear this.

She decides to speak as this seems never-ending. She gives up and begins conversing what are your hobbies? what do you do on weekends? favourite colours etc...

It becomes more like rhetorical she asking and he answering and he asks back the same question. ...it was good as Anaya knew the pattern.

For the first conversation with someone stranger, this was amazing.And somewhere she started to feel "Hari" might be that **Mr.Perfect** for her

There was the scope of the next meeting …this point was clear at the end of the meeting.

That night Anaya calls the twins to express her nervousness and flow of conversation. The twins feel confident that their Anaya is finally on track.

The next week she meets Siddarth in the supermarket and conveys she met a guy who seemed to match well.

Siddarth smiles widely congratulates and questions who was the guy what does he do to which Anaya shares the whole information on him.

That day Siddarth's face was a little off not sure why but before he left he conveyed Anaya to assess the guy once again ...since it's a sensitive matter.

That weekend, Hari and Anaya had to planned a date again. Both visited a restaurant .Anaya by now was comfortable she spoke about her trio group of friends and the first patient she saved in her initial days as intern who later became her close friend.

The gist of her being transparent was she trusts Hari and respects him as a person.

Hari also adds his stories to his friendship circle. Casually as they speak Hari randomly asks about her experience of saving her first patient as he notices that she was extremely proud of saving her first patient would want to talk more on that.

Hari : "Don't get me wrong! Can you tell me what did you do as a doc ?"

Just then **Siddarth** who was closely observing at another table from the time casually comes forwards and calls "Hey Anaya! What's up? ".

Anaya is shell shocked to see Siddarth in the same restaurant.

Anaya with surprise look on her face … "Heyy Sid! What a pleasant surprise.Meet Hari. And Hari, meet Siddarth…he is the same patient whom I saved :)".

Siddharth: "Ohh! Sorry, buddy! I guess I came at the wrong time :) so well yes you can see me the doc is excellent and I am fit, fine healthy Hahaha! You can trust her over her skills I bet you that."

Hari nods his head and smiles half-heartedly. The air was very not comfortable for him. He turns to Anaya and says "Anaya let's meet again another day. I got to rush have some pending things to wind "

Anaya and Siddarth bid farewell to him.Anaya notices relief in Siddarth's face. But Anaya has yet expectation from Hari that he is truly a perfect fit for her in many ways. She eagerly waits for the next meeting. But somewhere she is confused about Siddarth's behaviour that day.She keeps silence as she always felt when time is right she knew she would hear from him. She trusted Sid and this would never break.

Anaya by now gained experience and had started applying to other hospital in abroad as doctor as her expertise of interest could be nourished well in abroad. That day she got mail with offer letter of a big hospital in Chicago. She was supposed to start tentatively by next 20 days. But since she found her man she was sceptical about her life and career choices. She decided she would discuss this with Hari next time.She wanted to say about this news of she flying abroad to the twins personally while she missed time and again.A week later (Saturday) she decides that she has to call the twins and break this news.

That day, On TV, reports the arrest news of a spy "**Krishna**".Anaya in nurse station sees the TV connected. Her face showed that she was taken aback hearing news. Nurse Tina adds "Hello! Are you ok?". Anaya nods in agreement.

To Anaya's surprise, it was her blind date guy Hari Shetty. It was devastating to Anaya but at the same time a strange kind of satisfaction as well.She rushes home ...she calls both to come home that day ".Roohi and Pihu rush in the evening, worry written all over their face.Eager to hear and console Anaya.

The BIG Announcement

Anaya comes to her house to see Ruhi and Pihu already waiting eagerly. The trio sit on the sofa. There was an awkward silence among them which never happened before.Something was not in balance but the air wasn't awkward.

Roohi and Pihu hug Anaya to console her.

Anaya hugs back and wispers with contented smile that she was fine..She was someone who was most happy irrespective of everything that happened as she was saved from failed marriage.

Pihu: "Anaya, shouldn't we celebrate this victory of you being saved today…see the brighter side"

Anaya laughs "Pihu, you are just apt!! Infact we have to party! Ladies I am saved truly heavens are too good to me. So we have to party but before that ….I have something to tell you"

Anaya adds " So yes, Chitrakoots, I have some announcements that I want to make …

I have good and bad news but yes depends on what you perceive(gives a bright smile).......I am leaving this hospital and will not practice medicine here"… Shows offer letter from "Chicago University Hospital".She adds.." Ok I had got this offer letter long before, I was hesitant before and also when I felt Hari could be my man ..I felt my career aspiration could hold a break for sometime…but since I don't have that reason anymore thanks to Hari I can now follow my dream.. and guess what ? I will start being a amature book author as I always wanted to be one...so yes finally I am following my passion to write as well.... so yes girls! Let me make this clear that next week I am flying to States. And this decision is unchangeable please don't try to persuade me in any way. I wanted my Chitrakoots to understand !"

Ruhi and Pihu are dumbstruck and shocked and somewhere happy to hear this...

Ruhi :"Hey Anaya, what are you saying? Are you serious?"

Pihu adds "Why flying to abroad where we can't even watch over you ....it will worry us… why do you want to do all these to us ?"

Anaya adds "Heyy chills, I know I have a great backbone right next to me that is you guys!!. But hear me out I am not weak firstly. It's a choice that I want to make for myself"

Pihu adds "Come on!!!"

Ruhi adds "Shut up Pihu! Anaya, I don't agree.By the way did you discuss this with your parents. Did they agree ?"

Anaya adds " I haven't told yet, but I know my family will agree. It's my happiness is all they ask and I can assure that from my end. Why are you guys overacting? Ohhhoo Ruhi I am fine and I will be fine. And I promise you if I am not fine both of you will be the first ones to know that. Is that a deal ?"

Ruhi and Pihu half-heartedly look at each other and nod in agreement.

Pihu adds "What about Siddarth? Have you even thanked him? Had he not gatecrashed you other day by now you guys would be engaged and married too maybe. And what about this decision did you say to him ...even he cares you as much as us you should consult him too."

Anaya adds "Of course, I will thank him. It's even now !! I saved him and he saved me back we are free from being in gratitude. "

Ruhi and Pihu nod heads in agreement.

Sometimes your action speaks more than what you don't want to convey sometimes it hides what you have to tell.

Anaya's decision was somewhere between that edge.People say every decision has hidden meaning.What is the hidden meaning behind this is a big secret...Was she true to herself? Was she true to her friends? Was she true to Siddarth?.Anaya was wavered by Siddarth and she knew it.But she avoided as she felt she is right in controlling her emotions.

She had 101 reasons why she didn't want to let her heart go wild.Those 101 reasons were not just to control herself for society or others...somewhere it was "Does he feel what she feels? Are her feelings burdensome to him?...so on".That day was the last day she ever spoke about Siddarth.They say "When you love you should face the world ".But was her love really true love? Was it something so easy to getaway ? Was it not cowardly to behave?Or is this just one side of the coin?

The chapter Anaya as naive just a ordinary doctor ends here - Year 2015-Dec.

The Beginning of the End

In Anisha's house ,

Swara and Vani are dumbstruck by the ending of the story.It's almost 4 pm in the evening. Swara and Vani didn't realise it was almost time when Anisha would return from Hospital and Anika from school.

Swara : "She doesn't know even today. It's high time Siddarth opens up.....And that too it's so evident here that Anisha loved Siddarth ....as usual she doesn't confess back"

Vani :"Shut up Swara! It's too late now she has a family now."

Swara :" I should have told Anisha that day when I caught him in my showroom"

Vani :"Yes, he convinced us not to convey his identity or his love"

Swara :"I feel so responsible for this mess Vani. I wanted Anisha to express herself first but when Siddarth said he was also in love but Anisha doesn't I believed him. I should have known she always denies her feelings"

Swara :"Can we not say everything now ....everything he being a detective agent undercover ....he madly and secretly loving Anisha from the beginning.There are just so many things we didn't say about him to her look at the mess we did. I can't believe she loved Siddarth...Vani I regret it so much."

Vani: "Do you know where is Siddarth? But wait ….what is the use now what about Anu baby. No, we can't break a family ."

Swara :"Come on Vani! Siddarth will complete this family. Anika who never met her father will get a new one just like how Anisha experienced her motherhood with this orphan kid she was blessed to find other day.You never know Anu baby might bring them together too"

Swara and Vani always spoke on this topic in bits and pieces in the room whenever they visited Anisha ... as Anisha who stayed below couldn't hear anything that happens above. That's how they managed to decorate the terrace on her birthday the previous day "the birthday eve".

Anisha had come back around 1hr earlier and slowly eavesdropped on their conversation as it's was high time now the words of the floor above should be heard below...

A door creaks behind Swara and Vani .....as Anisha slowly pushes the door .....which distracts the duo inside the room ....they turn to face the door ......stand there dumbstruck.

Anisha smiles and adds "Now tell me what do you guys know about real Siddarth?"

Twins say together " Anisha.....!!!"(Soft whisper voice)

Swara : " I am so sorry ...not sure how should I ask forgiveness for hiding all these ....Forgive us once... we will bring back your happiness and find your Siddarth...but Anisha why didn't you tell that you loved him. You made us believe too....how are we supposed to untangle your mind...but either way we know it was wrong to keep it inhiding all these years."

Anisha smiles and giggles again "Ok I will answer all your questions .... We are even now. The book you are reading is not my novel The surrendered life....my novel is this. (Holds a book The surrendered life) "

Vani : " What! We saw the contents of past chapters it matched it's your biopic and we knew it anyway"

Anisha :" The story I told you is from this book your holding because that's my personal diary..the diary I maintained that's how I built passion for writing as well..my own story….my personnel journal inspired me to be a author…and yes ...I wanted you guys to look for the book that's the reason I wrapped it with my novel cover Surrendered life. And yes all thanks to the book review that happened other day . That day when I had been to review my novel I tried to express that every fictional character is me in that book because I am the creator and I have given life to my characters in the novel ..... but before I complete just like you both my Director misunderstood so the media... and they published that the book might be a biopic...This yellow news you guys believed which I took advantage of to know what did you guys know about Siddarth "

Vani and Rohi see each other's face in astonishment and smile contentedly..

Vani : "That means you made us look like fools... No wonder you didn't have copies of this novel and we searched complete house to find one ufff my god! Now tell me how much is the truth how much in this is your imagination I can't trust you now Anisha you might say that personal diary is my novel and novel is my biopic"

Anisha giggles again "Ok, I will clear the air for you guys! "

Anisha: "I knew that Siddarth didn't open anything in hospital .....when he was injured...the personality change that I saw when he was desperate about the number plate and then later when he dodged the same saying he wanted that number plate to find his long lost relative went too out of reach...you know when someone is closely watching you ...you can't really lie...I knew that Siddarth was sharing with me a mocktail of truth and his imagination...yet I didn't say anything...Later when he came to my date night and spoiled my day I realised maybe I should react the way he wanted and I knew this gate-crash was planned move. I knew there was something that he wants to tell but he can't express it.So I decided to follow his gestures act as he wants me to….And if he wanted to reach me I knew he can find me wherever I was I guess you agree with that as well for someone who give codes to say location to meet I can expect that definitely that's why I didn't tell him much just informed I would fly abroad and he nodded. Now you tell, I have assumed many things about him and he knows he never told I never asked as I felt it might hurt him but now that you guys know tell me what is the backstory of Siddarth.."

Swara begins "Yes, Anisha ...he didn't open anything to you but it was because he felt his feelings will be rather more burdensome to you...And we knew you that you weren't someone who would fall in love ....but our mistake we should have never assumed ....Anisha one brief word on who is Siddarth he is /was/will always be your soulmate ...he loved you may be to the point where he was already on cloud nine just by knowing you are fine...he was like that...And something that's more shocking is he is not Techie or Hacker ...he was an undercover detective agent who used to change his looks to get some national secrets ...and I found him in store accidentally that's how he revealed everything and told us not to tell you what he was and what his feelings were towards you..."

Swara, Vani and Anisha share every bit they knew about each other...

Vani and Swara narrated whole situation that happened on the day of Siddarth accident while Anisha slowly discloses her side of story to Vani and Swara

Flashback .....

On the day of the accident

Siddarth on the phone while rash driving on the local road .."Hello sir! This is '**Not me**' speaking. I have got the important leads on the terrorist gang who are planning to bomb Dharavi..." ...just as he crossed KitKat restaurant he was ambushed by a car who was from the same terrorist gang and Siddarth lost control. Siddarth was losing his breath and there was no one to call an ambulance. Just then a boy who was playing in front of his house noticed Siddarth and informed his mother who later took him to the same hospital where Anisha worked.

Once he was treated ...he was extremely impatient but unfortunately, he had forgotten the date and location details that he found out since he had slight edema which caused temporary memory loss ....he couldn't have waited till he regained back his memory ...that's when he asked Anisha what did he say to her when he was brought him.

Fortunately, Siddarth had conveyed the dates and location to Anisha in a code language which he knew how to decode ...to keep the secrecy .... Anisha felt it was a number plate and reported the numbers and Siddarth knew the details.

The following morning he had a meeting with the Defence ministry.Siddarth and his troupe were now well ready to face this ...Siddarth who was undercover officially watching movements as the common man.

But his plan went a little off track when he started to have feelings for Anisha and called her to the same restaurant where the accident took place.

The terrorist group member who was closely watching the area to find Siddarth .....found him with another woman.

The gang leader sent a man who could get details from Anisha assuming she would know about Siddarth as a marriage proposal to Anisha - That guy was the same blind date guy - Hari Shetty.

Anisha conveyed to Siddarth on the day of the first date that she had been on a blind date but the guy seems to be good. Siddarth feels a little off hence he follows Anisha on a second date to realise that the guy Anisha was interested in was part of the same terrorist group. He calls up his team and tells them to find some dirt around this guy to get him arrested temporarily at least so that Anisha breaks this relationship.

Siddarth realises that his presence was not safe for Anisha. As he knew why was she targeted.

Siddarth's team traps the following week that guy on a spying case. This comes up in the news of course without his name mentioned.

That night he left a text saying "Anisha, I will meet you one day maybe to be more than a friend... "

That was the last text he wrote and Anisha replies that coming week she would be flying to abroad. Siddarth reads and keeps quiet.

After another 4 months, Siddarth's success story of arresting terrorist gang was on paper but his name wasn't mentioned as he was always known for undercover activities.

Swara and Vani realised this since they knew the true face of Agent Siddarth.

In Anisha's house,

Vani and Swara are now curious about the journey after. Anisha answers every curiosity question that Swara had.

Anisha continues as if she was narrating the next sequel of her dairy.

Flashback....

Anisha journey as an author starts from here. Every book of hers has one mystery poem always on the last page.

Sun and moon never shy's away

In it's presence, it has its sway

dawn morning in orange chill

dazzling light has its own pride

amidst falling leaves and chilly night, it completes a day

roundabout tomorrow is new a beauty to shine again

the birds in the sky is a beauty that will never be a vain

come on all let's cherish to be here today

to see a new **paradise** on a calm **beach** and a clear sky!!

It was written to convey that Siddarth finds her on Paradise beach one day.

After one year Anisha's first book was published and in 6 months her next book. Every book had this poem she started gaining popularity through her books ....She was often questioned on the poem but she always dodged by saying it was a thanking note to mother nature.

After another year

One day, it was almost evening at 6 pm, Anisha receives a call from a number hears a soft voice "Anisha I am in Paradise"

Anisha is overjoyed to hear this she rushes to Paradise beach...

There he stands with around 2yr old girl holding one hand of Siddarth. Anisha slows down in astonishment thinking did he come to me with his daughter?

She goes towards him "Hey Siddarth, how are you ?"

Siddarth adds "Hey Anisha, I really don't know what shall I say to you? But yes I am happy to see you fine! "..tears roll out of his eyes . A blissful tear that spoke louder than any speaker "Yes, he is in ecstatic love"

Anisha smiles which covers her tears in her eyes and smile .Anisha wouldn't accept but yes the same Hindustani Naari of one day is in bliss …in ecstatic love with Siddarth.

Anisha :"I know Siddarth! I do know what you are as a person though I don't have a slight knowledge of what you do I know and understand that every lie you said had a truth that you felt I might not digest and I understood that!"

Anisha stops there was the briefest silence that touched the evening sky...

Anisha :"Don't say anything else I will never be able to muster the courage that I have now...just listen don't speak just listen...Siddarth I love you and this doesn't have to bind you or me to anything. To me love is freedom ...I am happy in just knowing the fact you are happy and we had spent time together even if that was brief it was all I need for all my life ."

Siddarth is dumbstruck to listen to Anisha confess ....in such an easy way.

Siddarth smiles naughtily :"Hey hey lady! Chills I wanted to do confession first you just spoiled it !! Hahaha! I love you too Anisha ... I expect nothing from you apart from your safety "

Siddarth slowly draws his hands back and adds "But I can't fulfil the dreams that you might be dreaming now. "brings the 2 yr kid in front saying yes I have many reasons but one among them is this kid too..."

Anisha: "What dreams? I don't have one. Ohh yes, And who is she? Such an adorable kid, you have got. Is she your daughter ? "

Siddarth adds "Yes, she is a daughter of someone... I found her on the road thrown and so I got her home and I am her guardian since then. So yes you can call me her sworn father. "

Anisha smiles and adds " What? I am so proud of you. Someone who is a rude hacker has a soft corner...So wait! Are you still ....?"

Siddarth adds "Yes, I am ....I can't love any other women ..Yet….yet…. I can't marry you. But Anisha you are the only lady in my life I can fulfil all responsibilities a man should do if he was his husband but I can't marry you.....(thinking of the fact how his movement brought Anisha in trouble last time) ...so .....Anisha, I came to tell you that you have to marry a guy who can love and yet marry you just like any normal couple which I can never do to you.."

Anisha understands the worrisome face he had at that movement.

Anisha adds "Heyy! I can't marry just anyone. Neither do I expect you to be with me as a partner. I told you... my love is not that you have to bargain with, it was to you and will always be to you. "

Siddarth adds "Anisha you got to be living in a beautiful family ....and you have to understand this won't be possible with me."

Anisha adds "Siddarth .....why do you think so your daughter is my daughter too... when you can be her sworn father ....then why can't I be her sworn mother..."

Siddarth has mixed emotions "Anisha! I hate that you don't have normal life you of all people I want you to be happy. Please understand!!!"

Anisha replies back stopping Siddarth "Wait up! I confirm being happy and what is this why and how am I having an abnormal life...when I have a daughter and daughter's father by my side. But just one thing I want you to do to me. Can you entrust your daughter in my hands? I shall be her mother. I will give that motherly love that you couldn't provide... she will be a reflection of you ....she will be my family Siddarth. Can I keep her with me in your name ? "

Siddarth : "Anisha ! (Happily) Really do you really want to do that ? Oh my god ! That's a big thing Anisha ! Are you sure "a girl is a responsibility" Anisha ."

Anisha adds "Why? All kids are the responsibility of elders. And I don't have any problem if you can support me when I need it :).So will you be a call away when I need? Just one thing please don't share with me some encoded messages I am not that smart now !!!.... Hahaha!"

Siddarth adds "Heyy! Docter! Indeed! Thank you, Docter! And yes if I say shows a paper that reads " **uoy evol I"** ….will you hit me? Hahaha!"

Anisha:" Yes, I will! (Laughs heartily) You and your code language !!"

Anisha : "Heyy! What is her name? Have you given one? ...please don't tell me you named her in some weird code language."

Siddarth :"Uhhhh....(laughs) No ...not exactly but I named her tweaking your name ...she is Anika. Ok I give up you can hit me for this ...(Hahaha)"

Anisha and Siddarth laugh heartily.Anisha slowly takes Anika's hand and takes her to the beach ...both play while Siddarth watches the sight with a look of extreme satisfaction of finding a family.

In Anisha's house,

Swara and Vani were in tears to hear this.

Swara turns to Vani and says "Heyy! Roohi did you ever think the rude women of our college days ever would be turning to this level...I always thought she doesn't believe in love .....but ...I was wrong ...this women's definition is quite something!!! .."

Vani smiles in satisfaction and in relief turns at Anisha : "I am proud of you both "

All 3 laugh ...

The 3 Chitrakoot holiday the next 5 days as planned and leave to their houses ...with biggest relief and mystery solved.

Nobody asked Anisha did they (both) meet again with Anika ... they knew whatever was to be done Anisha will take care of it.

Epitome of Love

Anisha's definition of love wasn't limited to religion, feelings, gifts, society, status . It was extreme understanding to the partner and trust. She never asked what did you do? why did you do that? why can't you marry me ?....because she knew she didn't need those as long as she knows her love.

Love is freedom to her. It is that unspoken comfort zone of each other.Love is above all ...above fights...marriage ....special days ....or sex...

Love is not even being with each other. It is just a friendly relationship and a joint responsibility of caring for each other without a government bond or certificate or blood relations.

Anisha was calm to hear Siddarth as he was an **Agent** all these days ...after 8 years ....she still had the same trust and this revelation wasn't going to change anything between them.

That weekend, Anisha goes to the same paradise beach with Anika ...

Sid comes after a while ..." Heyy Docter!! How are you? "

Anisha looks at him afar ...**Sid** adds "Heyy Anu baby! Your Sid pere(In french - Father) is here!"

Anu rushes to Sid and hugs him tightly ...adds "I missed you Sid pere! "

Sid hugs tightly :"I missed you too Anu baby I missed you so much ! love you baby"

Sid and **Anisha** sit on a rock ..Anisha turns toward Sid and looks into his eyes with confidence and pride of achieving something ....she says "For your information...I know that you are an undercover agent..... how do I know this I guess an undercover agent will be capable of guessing ....hahaha!!

This shocks Sid ....he adds "Ohh your Chitrakoots nothing stays hidden in you three I know.... so ....." with nervousness tone he waits for Anisha's reply.

Anisha laughs and adds "Yes you are right! I pranked them to make them splurt this .....and so...I am fine with it! And yes I understand why what, but and ifs of your perspectives with me and Anu...and yes irrespective of anything and everything .....my stance is still the same. We are happy! We are happy with you! And I wanted you to know that "

Sid smiles in contentment ...A brief silence covers the air ....A calmness hustled over the sea...

Sid adds "As a good friendship in your and my society our relationship has always been pure Anisha! ....But yes I am a little relieved though !! Hahaha! Next month same day I will meet you at the beach with Anika"

Sid adds "Ohh yes! Have you ever counted how many times we met? Monthly once ....so yearly 12 and it been 8 years ....12x8......And expense to come here all the way travelling miles together..to USA"

Anisha and Sid laugh heartily ...Anisha adds "Ohh please you are bad at maths stop Sid.Ofcourse! I am extremely high maintenance but don't blame me you fell in love with me ".

Anisha and Sid laugh heartily while Anu comes back with handful of sand and throws at these two to make them play with her….

Anisha and Sid chase Anika as she runs….The whole time is still as if even the setting sun doesn't want to set as if the sun is also moved by this "Purest form of love" .Indeed it was "Ecstatic Love".Indeed it was "Ecstatic Love"

A note to the reader :

Sometimes you might feel Sid could have just told his profession upfront ...but he wasn't comfortable to do so ...Sid could have probably expressed ... He didn't find it right to say but somewhere he believed Anisha would understand the fact why he didn't share complete truth.

Had he said everything truth do you think things would be any different ...maybe.. may not be ...Anisha could have asked that why couldn't he trust her but she didn't because she wanted to hear from Sid only those things which he could transparently say....now that Sid has confidence either he lies or says truth it will be understood in all circumstances ...this statement Anisha wanted to convey and she conveyed beautifully.

Love is being comfortable with each other, isn't it?

Does it need any limits or bounds? Maybe not ..at least in this story...of course, every love story has its own beauty ...every lover has their own definition of love .....hence people portray love as abstract ...and invincible...That is why it's "Surreal" .A relationship with love and later marriage are normal stories that many hear or read. Yes, here it's not normal too. It takes a lot of guts to be abnormal. This story is hence a cocktail of fantasy of an ecstatic love

Here it ends **"SURREAL TALE"**

"A TALE OF LOVE"

"A TALE OF FRIENDSHIP"

"A TALE OF A BEAUTIFUL LIFE"

-End-

The truth behind the names :

- **Vani - Speech and Swara - Syllable. The twins complete each other**

- Roohi and Pihu are the nicknames of the twins which was given by Anisha

- Roohi meant **music tone that touches the heart** ...to Anisha, Vani(Childhood name - Roohi) is an all-time Music ie; comfortable company and Pihu meant **Chatting bird** when **Swara** (Childhood name – Pihu) **is around she makes the room noisy with her squeaky voice**

- Anaya name was given by the twins.**Anisha** was the **leader of this trio to create chaos and pranks**. Hence the name **Anisha**(Childhood name -Anaya) **which meant without a superior**

About the Author

Avani was born on 3rd Aug 1997 in South India, Udupi whose roots follow the coastal areas of Karnataka.Growing up she was passionate about writing poems which nourished her free time to not just free time but peaceful time.She has graduated as Information Science Engineer from Bangalore Institute of Technology, Bangalore.She works as Software Engineer hence forth. Since she was a hobbyist writer from her childhood, she continued her momentum and this book is her first venture to outside world to showcase her thoughts. She is a blogger and calls her readers as wings.Her blog posts always end with #WingsToMyThoughts indicating her readers form the support to fly high as a writer.Lastly, Avani is her pen-name, her official name is "VAIDEHI".

Connect with Avani

I really appreciate you reading my book! Here are my social media coordinates:
Subscribe to my blog : https://urwordsfelt.wordpress.com/author/avani97/
Subscribe to my youtube : https://www.youtube.com/channel/UCGwfu33_8UwcFQedNqP5gtQ

Printed by Libri Plureos GmbH in Hamburg,
Germany